For James

First U.S. edition 2015

Library of Congress Catalog Card Number 2014949721
ISBN 978-0-7636-7958-3

15 16 17 18 19 20 TWP 10 9 8 7 6 5 4 3 2 1

Printed in Johor Bahru, Malaysia

This book was typeset in Times New Roman Regular.
The illustrations were done in ink and watercolor.

TEMPLAR BOOKS

an imprint of
Candlewick Press
99 Dover Street
Somerville, Massachusetts 02144
www.candlewick.com

Sam Usher

SNOW

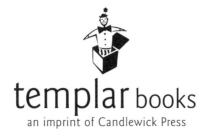

templar books
an imprint of Candlewick Press

When I woke up
this morning, it
was snowing!

I couldn't wait to
go to the park.

All I needed to do was dress,

brush my teeth, put my shoes on,

and get Granddad.

We had to get outside
in the snow . . .

before anyone else.

I was ready to go,
but Granddad wasn't.

I said, "Don't forget about
the snow!"

And he said,
"Don't forget your scarf."

So we weren't quick enough to be first.

Granddad was taking forever.
So I shouted,

"All the others will
get there first, Granddad!
DON'T FORGET
ABOUT THE SNOW!"

And Granddad said,
"Don't forget
your hat!"

So we weren't quick enough
to go with my friends.

Granddad was taking **forever.**
So I shouted,

"HURRY UP,
GRANDDAD!"

And he said,
"It's OK, we're not
going to miss
the fun."

But we were! I told him all the cats and dogs were out there.

Granddad laughed and said the whole zoo
was probably out there.

And then I saw something. . . .

I did!

Finally, Granddad was ready.

We headed to the park.

Where I could play in the snow at last.

We played all the games you can play in the snow.

Granddad won the snowball fight
six slushings to four.

So I think he had fun too.

Back at home,
Granddad and
I agreed that
some things are
definitely worth
waiting for.

I hope it snows
again tomorrow.

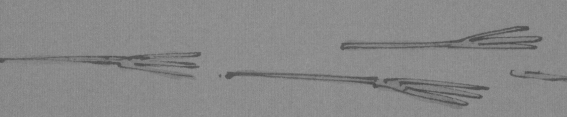